SERIES EDITOR: ANNE HARVEY

POETRY ORIGINALS

The Magnificent Callisto

by Gerard Benson

Illustrated by Cathy Benson

Blackie Children's Books

BLACKIE CHILDREN'S BOOKS

Published by the Penguin Group
Penguin Books Ltd, 27 Wrights Lane, London W8 5TZ, England
Penguin Books USA Inc., 375 Hudson Street, New York, New York 10014, USA
Penguin Books Australia Ltd, Ringwood, Victoria, Australia
Penguin Books Canada Ltd, 10 Alcorn Avenue, Toronto, Ontario, Canada M4V 3B2
Penguin Books (NZ) Ltd, 182–190 Wairau Road, Auckland 10, New Zealand

Penguin Books Ltd, Registered Offices: Harmondsworth, Middlesex, England

First published 1992
1 3 5 7 9 10 8 6 4 2

Introduction copyright © 1992 Anne Harvey
Text copyright © 1992 Gerard Benson
Illustrations copyright © 1992 Cathy Benson

The moral right of the author and illustrator has been asserted

Printed in Great Britain by Butler and Tanner Ltd, Frome and London

A CIP catalogue record for this book is available from the British Library

ISBN 0216 93267 X

Contents

The Magnificent Callisto is Gerard Benson's first collection of poems for children, although he has been involved with poetry for a long time. He was born in 1931 and, when he was eight, the Second World War began. It was about that time the first 'real' poem caught hold of him: William Blake's 'The Tyger'. Gerard Benson says of the poem, 'It works its magic on me still, just as it did when I was little. Lines like

"When the stars threw down their spears,
And watered heaven with their tears . . ."

are really beyond understanding, but then they had a clear meaning for me. I thought it was just like when you had been crying and could see through your tears lines of silver coming from the stars, linking heaven and earth.'

Parts of other famous poems had a similar power and beauty for Gerard, for example, the first few lines of Shelley's 'Ode to the West Wind': 'O wild west wind, thou breath of Autumn's being . . .' Another great poet, William Wordsworth, was spoilt for him, though. When Gerard read the lines

'I wandered lonely as a cloud
That floats on high o'er vales and hills . . .'

he imagined the cloud was like one of the war-time barrage balloons, all grey and floppy, and he had the strange idea that William Wordsworth also resembled a barrage balloon!

Gerard went to a school called Rendcomb, an unusual school where the pupils were given a certain amount of independence. There were committees to settle disputes, and all the meetings were organised by the pupils. One teacher in particular, Gerard's Sixth Form teacher, Kathleen James, especially inspired them. She had the gift of being able to show how to explore the author's meaning in a piece of writing — a lesson that still proves valuable.

After a year at Exeter University Gerard decided to leave and try his luck as an actor and says that he 'talked himself into' his first job. In 1960 he joined The Barrow Poets, a group of actors, musicians and poets who presented programmes in pubs, theatres and schools, in fact anywhere an audience could gather to see them: in the street, on a barrow, in churches (including Westminster Abbey), village halls, and private homes. It was in one of these performances that I first saw him.

If your life and work experience is varied it means you have a wide variety of experience to draw ideas from if you become a writer. As well as acting, Gerard has taught all age groups, including students in a drama college. He has been a story teller, a book reviewer, and editor. He has run writing workshops for adults and children, and has given readings in schools and colleges, as well as in the British Museum. He is also what he himself calls a 'comper', defined as 'a person who regularly enters literary competitions' (and in his case, it seems, usually wins them) under various 'noms de plume' so that the judges won't say 'Oh, no, not him again!'

Gerard is an expert in riddles, crosswords, puzzles and puns: all types of wordplay. A good example comes in the poem 'Tapestry' in this collection. Not only is it based upon a 'sestina' (an intricately patterned verse form with verses of six lines each), but it is also based upon a word game in which you must change one word into another by altering one letter at a time. I'll tell you that in the first verse, 'wind' becomes 'rain' in this way: wind – wand – land – laid – raid – rain. Now, work out the rest for yourself.

On 29th January 1986, Gerard and two friends launched the project Poems on the Underground, a real inspiration for London Transport tube travellers who can now read poems to enliven their journeys. The first hundred poems were published in 1991 and the book includes a thousand-year-old riddle, translated by Gerard from the Anglo Saxon:

> A moth, I thought, munching a word,
> How marvellously weird! a worm
> Digesting a man's sayings—
> A sneakthief nibbling in the shadows
> At the shape of a poet's thunderous phrases—
> How unutterably strange!
> And the pilfering parasite none the wiser
> For the words he has swallowed.
> (Answer: Bookworm)

It was also during 1991 that Gerard won the Signal Poetry Award, a prize given annually for excellence in the field of poetry. He won it for his unusual and original anthology *This Poem Doesn't Rhyme*, a marvellous treasure chest to dip into; no rhymes, but a richness of ideas, vocabulary, rhythm, alliteration — all the elements of poetry.

It is because I knew him to be so enthusiastic and caring in his approach that I was excited when he agreed to be one of the first poets on the Blackie Poetry Originals list. You will find a range of poems from him — sad, funny, truthful, fantastic; you will find out that cucumbers were once known as 'earth-apples', that 'Araneus Diadematus' is the real name for the ordinary brown garden spider, that there are more birds in East Africa than you ever dreamed about. And in the last poem of all you'll discover that typewriters can get quite out of control and release the craziest words while the poor poet cries for 'Hlep!' Perhaps the poet's wife, Cathy Benson, will come to his rescue. She's certainly brought his poems to life with the most inspired illustrations. Cathy is a fine poet herself, and they have been married since 1984, having between them five grown-up children and three grandchildren.

Earlier I mentioned the first 'real' poem that Gerard Benson enjoyed. All the poems in *The Magnificent Callisto* are real poems, all here to work their different kinds of magic.

ANNE HARVEY

The Cat and the Pig

Once, when I wasn't very big
I made a song about a pig
    Who ate a fig
    And wore a wig
And nimbly danced the Irish jig.

And when I was as small as THAT
I made a verse about a cat
    Who ate a rat
    And wore a hat
And sat (you've guessed) upon the mat.

    And that, I thought, was that.

But yesterday upon my door
I heard a knock; I looked and saw
    A hatted cat
    A wiggèd pig
    Who chewed a rat
    Who danced the jig
    On my door mat!

They looked at me with faces wise
Out of their bright enquiring eyes,
'May we come in? For we are yours,
Pray do not leave us out of doors.
We are the children of your mind
Let us come in. Be kind. Be kind.'

So now upon my fireside mat
There lies a tireless pussy cat
Who all day long chews on a rat
    And wears a hat.
And round him like a whirligig
Dancing a frantic Irish jig
Munching a fig, cavorts a big
    Wig-headed pig.

They eat my cakes and drink my tea.
There's hardly anything for me!
And yet I cannot throw them out
For they are mine without a doubt.

But when I'm at my desk tonight
I'll be more careful what I write.

I'll be more careful what I write.

Fetching the Coal

I

The Coalmen

When the coalmen came,
We counted the sacks into the house,
Loud in our childish voices: One, Two, Three . . .
Fifteen, Sixteen, chanting together. It was big,
Our cellar, and deliveries were rare.

Like peculiar hooded monks,
Bowed from the heavy loads they carried,
(Each sack above fifty kilos of knobbly lumps)
Another sack folded sideways over back and head,
They trudged the coal in, through the kitchen,
To tilt and dump it onto the cellar floor.

II

The Coal Cellar

Lit by a low-watt bulb,
Our cellar held a tang that filled the lungs.

The largest lumps were marvellous to pick up
Between the hands, rough, shiny,
Complicated, like small black cliffs,
Landscapes of ridge and ledge.

Dark glittering dust which grimed my boots
Silted the dank stone floor.

III

Fetching the Coal

Shovelling it into scuttles,
A scraping dig into the pile
Brought small lumps tumbling,
A river of black jewels.

This time spent loading
The scuttles and buckets
Was good time,
Alone in the reeking dark
Imagining dinosaurs.

IV

Aunty Jane's Drawing Room

A gleaming Roman helmet
Filled with small coals,
Hand-picked and neatly piled,
Gives back the fire's golden flicker.

Beside it stands a small tree,
Its dangling fruit, a poker,
A dainty pair of tongs, a brush,
And a tiny brass shovel,
Polished like a mirror,
In which I can see my knees.

V

Watching the Fire

The coals gave up their heat,
Glowed and rippled
With many-coloured flames,
Red or yellow, or eerie blue.

Pictures emerged, faces,
Cities of mystery, migrant herds;
Or animated stories slowly evolved,
Which a sharp prod with the poker
Could destroy or alter.

VI

Ashes

How pale they were in the morning,
Like the faces in school
After a scared night in the air-raid shelters.

But sometimes when you dug
In the cold remains of last night's fire,
You would discover tiny hot splinters of rose.

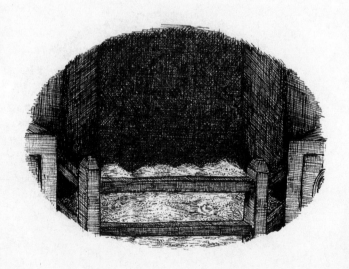

Stone

A firm fistful, earth-coloured,
This dull stone weights my arm —

Savage men on the uplands,
Pounders of skulls and grain —

With one hand I hold history,
Write with the other.

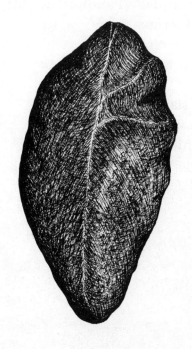

Scarecrow

A white disgusting scarecrow
Is eating a small stone
At the hilly end
Of a windy field.

His tattered coat
Flaps like a battle flag,
Slaps and bangs
Like washing on a line.

His head is a big round turnip,
Partly eaten away
By the birds
He was put there to scare.

He stares out over his field
Chewing away, chewing
At his little stone,
Lonely as a rake handle.

And the great black crows
Fly here and there,
Then strut across the furrows
Digging, digging.

The scarecrow
Digests the little stone
And stands straight as a soldier
As the rain begins.

February 5th 1940

Hedges were huge and hostile,
Mist was clammy cold;
Dreading the village school
I trudged along. The war
Was in its early months
And I was eight years old;
I'd never, ever walked
A country lane before.

The school had naked walls
From which an oil-lamp hung.
Our hair was raked for nits
With sharp and scratchy combs;
And at our desks that day
We wore our coats, and sang,
'Somewhere Over the Rainbow',
Thinking of our homes.

Molligan's Rock

Tom, basking on the sunny rock,
    Saw wavering people, very long,
    And heard far-off the wild sea song
And the rock was smooth and the rock was hot.

The goldpenny sun grew huge and fat
    And the salt sea's voice sang round and warm
    A murmurous song of distant storm
But the rock was high and the rock was hot.

All through the afternoon he sat
    And the castles stood till the tide poured through
    And the shimmering light of the long day grew
Round the rock so flat, the rock so hot.

Poets at Killiney

On a grey beach, on a grey afternoon,
  Three poets.

One, intent on dwindling into the distance,
Dwindles slowly into the distance.
Perfecting the trick, practised since
Childhood, of becoming a speck on the horizon.

One ranges between foam-edge and high-water
Quartering for booty: shells and stones.

One removes his shoes, dabbles his feet
And ankles in the cold ocean; and, after,
Sits on the hard grey pebbles and begins
To write a poem — this poem.

If You Knelt in the Mud

If you knelt in the mud
Down by Dolby's Pond
Under the little bridge
Where the slow water
Comes trickling in,
The knobs of your knees
And the fronts of your socks
And the tops of your shoes
Got coated with a soft blacky mixture,
Delicious to smell.
And you felt yourself gradually
Sucked downward
Into a sort of clammy
Heaven for the shins.

If you were still,
You could see fish
Gliding in well-behaved schools
And frogs, beautiful swimmers,
Tiny champion athletes
Displaying their perfect breast-stroke.

You could hear the riddles of the river
And a choir of pond voices
And secret rustlings that told you
Something small was moving, somewhere.

The big willows dangled their trailing branches
Into the water; ducks patrolled;
Moorhens looked busy. And you believed
Everything would always be the same.

And when you went home
The mud caked and dried
On your knees and socks and shoes.
It crumbled and flaked off.
You were a disgrace to look at
And you promised that next time . . .
Next time, you would come straight home.
Or remember your gum boots
Or take your shoes and socks off.
And the tin bath was brought to the kitchen fire
And you undressed and got in and you hoped
That not too many neighbours
Would suddenly drop by.

And next time . . . next time,
If you were very still, you might be lucky
And see a grey heron
Standing statue-like at the water's edge
Or watch its great umbrellas open
As it lazily crossed to the small island;
Or you might learn the tune
The reeds were whistling.

Boy on a Bicycle

When I pedal my bicycle along the lanes
    Or take a hill with dizzying speed,
I seem to myself not a boy on a bike, but a bird
    Flying, or a cloud scudding. As if freed
For a while from the weightiness of earth, I fly
    And feel the air whizz past my face
And flap my shirt about my ribs.
    I know the delight of movement, the power of pace.

But oh, the hills! The climbing. The pressing
    Downward to rise. The effort. The thick ache
In the legs, as I stand on the turning pedals,
    Zagging from side to side. Determined to make
The top. And failing. And dismounting. And heavily
    Wheeling the machine. No bird. An ordinary boy,
Till at last I reach the highest point
    And again race downward in a new discovery of joy.

Play No Ball

What a wall!
Play No ball,
It tells us all.
Play No Ball,
  By Order!

Lick no lolly.
Skip no rope.
Nurse no dolly.
Wish no hope.
Hop no scotch.
Ring no bell.
Telly no watch.
Joke no tell.
Fight no friend.
Up no make.
Penny no lend.
Hand no shake.
Tyre no pump.
Down no fall.
Up no jump.
Name no call.
  And. . .
Play No Ball.
No Ball. No Ball.
  BY ORDER!

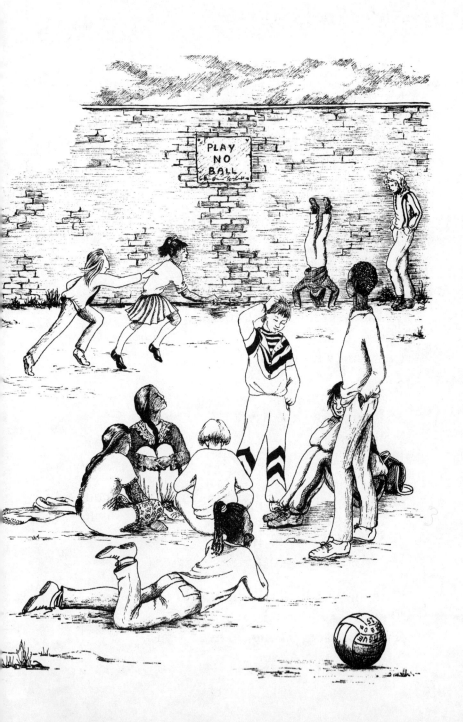

Algie's Trick

My friend Algie told me to think of a number,
So I thought of three,
(Useful for triangles
And three-legged stools).

'Double it,' he said,
So I doubled it. Two threes are . . .
Six,
(What the egg man calls half a dozen).

'Add on four,' my friend said,
So I added four. Six and four are . . .
Ten,
(Just handy for my fingers).

'Halve it,' said Algie,
So I took away one hand.
Half of ten is . . .
Five.

'And now take away the number you first thought of,'
he said,
So I took three away from five . . .
'And the answer is two!' he said.

'Brilliant!' I said. 'How did you know that?'
'It always is,' said Algie.
'But supposing I'd chosen five?' I said.
'Still two,' said Algie.

So I tried it.
Five doubled is ten . . .
Add on four is fourteen . . .
Halve it, is seven . . .
And take away the number you first thought of . . .
Two again!

Then I tried it with thirty-seven thousand,
Eight hundred and forty-two and a half.
It took ages !
And would you believe it?!?!
The answer was two!

And when I tried it on Grandad,
The answer was *still* two.
'What number did you choose, Grampa?' I asked.
'I never chose a number,' he said, 'I chose a letter.'
'What do you mean?'
'I chose X.'
'X?'
'Yes.'
'What do you mean?'

'Well,' he said, 'X . . .
Double it, you've got two Xes . . .
Add on four, you've got two Xes and four . . .
Halve it, you've got one X and two . . .
Take away the X and you've got . . .'
'TWO!' I shouted.

It made me think.

Matthew

Bent and old as he is, Matthew Harbour
   Knows a thing or two,
And for the price of a leisurely talk
   He'll tell them to you.

'I have lived in this one house all my life,
   And since I first begun,'
He says, 'water's run under that there bridge,
   Bubbling on and on.'

'Never be people again,' he says, 'who've seen
   The changes I've seen. Born
Before there were cars; now they orbits the stars.
   They call it a New Dawn.'

His face creases like a crumpling page
   As he winks at you.
'So long as I've been alive,' he says,
   'Every dawn was new.'

The Day My Father Died

The day my father died
A huge dark cloud
Rolled slowly over Berkeley Hill.
My uncles walked across the fields
From Rudcombe. I see them still,
In their dark, tight suits,
Their heavy feet dragging in the clay,
Three large men, in line abreast,
Outlined against the green.
And suddenly
The swirling rise
Of a flock of starlings
Against the sky's pewter grey.

I.M. Patricia O'Brien

My cousin died
In New End Hospital
One starry night in June.
That very day
I'd been to visit her —
Against the rule
No Children in the Ward —
But matron let me stay.

My hump-backed Patsy,
Propped between two pillows,
Her skin like tracing paper,
Spoke with pain,
Sent each word
On its separate voyage.
Like moths her blue hands
Fluttered on the counterpane.

I'd no idea
Of what to say to her
There in the Women's Ward
But stood and saw
How easily a person
Shrinks to nothing;
Patsy, so little left
Of what she'd been before.

The Magnificent Callisto

Callisto cuts the cards
Using a sharp blade;
Doves fly out of his eyes.

A lady in glittering tights
Vanishes; in her place
Multitudinous stars

Play waltzes on little flutes.
Callisto conjures the King of Spades,
The swagged curtain stirs.

Now the show can truly commence!

There is a ball that hovers in the air;
There are pink fish that swim through glass;
There are artificial falls, that drop

Making trickles of tiny diamonds
On Callisto's assistant's cheeks.
Listen to the applause!

Now watch as the parts
Of the sawn-in-half man
Dance on the stage's boards,

Through which, predictably, spring
Flowers, spring flowers.
And then the curtain falls.
And then the curtain calls.

The Busker

His elbow jerks, an old mechanical toy.
Feet planted astride, knees flexed, one instep
Arched over the cobbles, he scratches a tune
From a bony violin, grating the spine.

His left hand, a dancing spider, performs
Its polka on the taut web strings, his right,
Daintier than a lady taking tea,
Guides the thin bow in dangerous little stabs,

Littering the yard with snips and snaps of sound,
Sharper than pins. Coins drop into his hat,
But sparingly, and pigeons on pink unhurried feet
Waddle, chatting by; refuse, point-blank, to dance.

Butterfly Boy

Summer afternoon. Simon sits outside
In permanent observation of antics
Of butterflies, flickering blue patterns
Across his wilderness of mindless amazement,
Nameless shreds of sky crazily
Careening in frantic and unmeaning behaviour.

Simon watches. And smiles. Cannot manage hands.
Simon watches. Butterfly detaches from perch on
         flower
And is a portion of blue iris
Liberated from stalk and leaf
Thriftlessly hurling (petals and one stamen)
Against grass and green its frailty.

Simon sees. And smiles. Cannot account for,
Can enjoy skyborne tatters of weightless blue
As the day shines sun, spilling over his life
A golden gladness. Can applaud a part of time
Which sends flowers that fly; sky that flakes
And scatters in fragments of pure laughter.

Tea with Léone

High summer and all
around her lavender bush
white butterflies
are dancing. We

sit and drink
lemon tea. Our
words among the tea things
dance like the butterflies,

lifting and falling,
rarely still.
Fifteen or twenty
white butterflies

flicker about the tall
sweet-scented shrub.

A visitor departs;
the iron gate squeals shut
and sketches its narrow
shadow on the brief grass, beginning with lean
dark bars to stripe
the lavender round whose small
misty blue flowers

the eternal
white butterflies dance
and dance. It seems
important to remember this.

The Wall

Lichen, a thumbprint, a golden stain
Bites into this limestone.

An intricate little rug of moss takes hold.
The lizard's home. Not old

This ramshackle barrier between
Your house and mine,

But already it stands its ground,
Refuses to be owned.

Next year, perhaps, the first flowers —
But the wall's, not ours.

Glendalough

And still the green, folding in from the wooded
                                        hillsides,
The birch leaves and the oak leaves green;
The green grass, starred with tiny white flowers
And small buttercups. Green.
And the dense light from the conifers,
Green. And the quiet slopping lake water muddy
                                        green.

Bark of trees, footworn path are brown;
Twigs brown. The fragile generous blackberry
                                        blossom
Pale in the green and brown. Butterflies
Brown, with spotted wings, white like the bramble
                                        blossom.

And still the waters reflecting the hillside
Green until all the summers have gone away
While the butterflies like little strobes
Rifle the blossom and then lurch away.

Tapestry

Damp pennants scarcely shift in the slow wind,
Each droops and wavers on its angled wand
A strange, unwholesome chill covers the land,
By an old Dragon-spell malignly laid.
Armed horsemen ride out on a vengeful raid,
And all that pictured plain is washed with endless rain.

Onward the riders spur their mounts; the rain
Enters their coats of mail, urged by a wind,
An eldritch blast which strives to thwart their raid,
Conjured, perhaps, by a hostile wizard's wand.
It terrifies their steeds, whose ears are laid
Back on their heads. This band rides reckless through
the land.

They ride the flowery fields of Fairyland
On shortened stirrup and on slackened rein.
Against a dark princess their schemes are laid,
Who ever in her tower a song unwinds,
And wreathes enchantments with a speckled wand.
It is against this maid these riders mount their raid.

Against this Dame in mystic robes arrayed,
Who dwells exiled, far from her dear homeland;
Against her clarsach and her magic wand,
Wherewith by song and spell she conjures rain,
They ride, these sharp-faced offspring of the wind.
Against this virgin maid their louting plans are laid.

Harsh plans, which for all time shall be delayed.
The chanting lady and the murderous raid
Are trapped in time. Watch, now, the river wind
Moveless across the grey and silent land.
There is no motion in the wind or rain,
No stir in fern or frond; all stilled by Merlin's wand.

All halted by the old magician's wand.
None of these griefs shall ever be allayed.
For all time stands the tower in the rain.
The horsemen gain no footfall in their raid.
No leaf decays. No shoot pierces the land.
The dark princess is limned by needle-strokes of wind.

The wand that first invoked this hopeless raid,
Is laid aside; nought stirs in that bleak land
But rain, hard driven by a sourceless wind.

Earth-apples

When I read in my old book
That in this island, long ago,
They ate cucumbers,
Calling them earth-apples,
I don't know why,
But my heart jumped for joy.

Now with my summer meals
I eat apples of the earth
In cool round slices,
And share the Garden of Eden
With a poet who lived
One thousand years ago.

Shriek of the Shrike

I beg your pardon, sir,
I could not help overhearing
Your sentimental words.
This is *my* garden, sir.
I am not singing but sneering
At those foolhardy birds
Trespassing by that tree:
Dusky turtle doves, a-pacing,
Cooing and strutting round.
They reckon without me.
Excuse me. It's time for chasing
Them off. This is *my* ground.

Birds in East Africa

Remembering that place, I see again
Dark chanting goshawk, maribou, crowned crane,
The shrike from which the dusky turtle dove
Fled for his life, the drongo, and above,
Three black kites wheeling, quartering for prey:
Then with its croaky call of 'Go away!'
The children's joke, white-bellied turaco;
The pratincole, the ostrich, the pied crow,
And, running in the trees, that longtailed clown
The crested mousebird; hanging upsidedown
The yellow weavers, sociable flocks,
Threading their high-rise stacks of nests like blocks
Of flats; jacana; brown and white fish eagle
Hunting by Lake Naivasha, huge and regal;
Nubian nightjar, ibis, guinea fowl,
Goliath heron,mournful eagle owl.

If the above is not enough,
I also saw the chough (or ruff?),
Oxpeckers on a buffalo,
Buzzards, the Indian house crow
(Down at the coast, shot as a pest),
The hamerkop who builds a nest
Too large for use, the lilac-breasted
Roller, bulbuls, and a crested
Eagle feeding on a rat,
Bee-eaters, sunbirds, a cliffchat,

A firefinch (size of a man's thumb,
Known as the 'animated plum'),
Swallows assembling for migration,
And like a pink hallucination,
Flamingoes by the thousand; these,
And storks which roost high in the trees.

Long-tongued Bat

They ride the air, pig-snouted things,
   Monsters from some weird Halloween;
Thin, angled bones define the wings
   Like Leonardo's flight machine.
This nightmare beast, this flickering spectre
Prickles my spine — yet feeds on nectar.

The Dragon and the Author

The writer's pen moved and the dragon, all
But tamed, waddled his innocuous way
Through the dull pages of a vacuous tale
Beaming at kids and giving rides, while they
Well-washed and pretty, waved from his ridged back
Prised fingers in between his tender scales;

But sometimes you might capture just a look,
Rapt, secret, in the eyes of a boy or girl
Who rode, as though the ancient furnace smouldered
                                              still
Beneath their bodies. If this was so, none spoke.
But some were found who strangely danced one day
And while they danced, the rumbling dragon's smoke
Rose high above the ruined citadel
Spelling old runes across the silent sky.

And when the writer started Chapter Twelve
And slowly spelled the dragon's secret name
The paper swiftly crackled into flame
And from the flame there rose an acrid smell.
Devouring teeth clashed on the moving quill
A cavernous mouth engulfed the writer whole
And drew him down into the reeking bowel.

The Dragon Speaks

I knew I was the last of the line
That the continuance of dragonkind
Depended on me but thought I was safe.

We were (or rather, I was)
A protected species,
And since I was extremely pregnant
(expecting a clutch within the century)
I was escorted everywhere
By the RSPCMB.*

That doomed day I was being exercised
In the Mythical Beings' Sanctuary
By a nice but gormless girl volunteer
When out of nowhere it seemed
Galloped this psychopath,
A butcher called George
Disguised in the insignia
Of the International Red Cross
But dressed underneath to kill
In an iron suit.

He thundered straight at me,
Lance to the fore.
I'd no time to dodge. (Well, I wasn't expecting
                                    anything)
And my wings were clipped so I couldn't fly
(Besides there was no room for take-off).
I spat a little fire
But only singed his horse.

Then he hit me,
Clean between the ventral plates.
Then pain.
Then planets in a dance.
Then darkness.

The rest is mythology.

*Royal Society for the Prevention of Cruelty to Mythical
Beings*

Alison's Dream

In the deep of the night she dreamed of dragons,
Ferocious monsters, fearsomely flying,
Sailing through the sky all wreathed in smoke,
Roaring as they ranged the air's upper reaches.

Terror-struck, she twisted in her tangled bedsheets,
Gasping for breath, her brow burning,
Till shuddering, she awoke, sheened with sweat,
Staring into the darkness, her soul stricken,
Oppressed by the power of the nightmare's presence.

She called for a candle (but no-one came),
Attended anxiously the arrival of light,
Waited awhile till dawn lit the window;
Not till then did she shake off the noisome night-vision.
Dazed with relief she donned her day clothing.

Then she found on the floor a triple-clawed footprint.

The Man in the Bowler Hat

'It's rare indeed to meet a Unicorn.
I only met him three times in my life.'

He wore a bowler, sitting in the park
And blinked his pale blue eyes through bottle glasses:
He had an ugly lump upon his back
That seemed to tilt him forward on the bench.

'Just three,' he said, folding his paper. 'Aye.
First time, of course, I thought myself mistaken.
But there was no mistaking that proud profile.
The grace, the mane that flowed like molten silver.
He wasn't white, but grey — a stippled flank;
He stood quite still in the half-light of a thornwood.
I knew he'd seen me. When I glanced away, he'd gone.'

'The second time, I saw him through a window,
Through glass and glass. He trotted in the snow,
Quite frisky, like a colt. But — this is strange —
He left no footprints and he threw no shadow.
His grey sides smoked; his fleshy nostrils flared,
Pink, tender, like a sea-anemone;
His horn shone in the mid-day sun. Third time,
(That was the best) I rode the Unicorn.'

'You never did.' I said. 'Oh aye,' said he.
'One sunrise, travelling in the Cumbrian hills.
I'd just come through a coppice when I saw him.
Drinking, he was. A mist rose from the ground.
The grass was wet. I talked him sweet and trod
Slowly to where he drank. He raised his head.
He looked me in the eye, and I at him.
I draped my scarf over his neck, then sprang
Onto his back. He stood and sniffed the air,
Then cantered off, snorting across the field.
I kicked his sides and bellowed for pure pleasure.
He moved into a gallop like the wind.
My finest moment but it didn't last.
He reared and threw me off into the ditch.
Then jumped the hedge and vanished in the mist.
That's when I hurt my shoulder, son,' he said.

The park was full of people. He stood up.
'I lost that scarf,' he said. He turned and went.
Limped swiftly off. I wanted to shout out,
To ask him more, but I was dumb. I saw
His bowler hat bobbing among the crowd.

Of course, he kept quite neatly to the path.
In our park there are signs: Keep Off the Grass.

The Hobby Horse

The hobby horse lies forgotten in the attic;
The uncle who made the beautiful hobby horse is far
  away;
The boy who rode the horse, tugging the reins as the
  wild mane flowed in the wind, has grown up.
The uncle who carved the noble wooden head is far, far
  away.
The toy horse lies forsaken in the attic.

But listen!
Can you hear the distant thunder of hooves?

Three Birds

Three birds flew in a clouded sky.
One was you and one was I
   And no-one knows the other.

The sky was heavy, soft and warm,
And off we flew to cheat the storm,
   You, I and the other.

To cheat the storm, away we flew;
One was white and one was blue.
   A raven was the other.

We flew to far-off countries, where
Soft waters speak to brittle air,
   Always with the other.

And there we bathed in silver springs
And shook the water from our wings;
   And with us came the other.

And in those fair, enchanted lands,
We built our nest upon the sands;
　　And still with us the other.

And when we sang, the trilling notes
Like liquid, rippled from our throats;
　　He never sang, that other.

Three birds mount toward the sun;
One is you, and I am one
　　And no-one knows the other.

Buffalo of the Plains

I saw him in the zoo,
The prairie buffalo —

A disconsolate creature
Like a street corner lounger.

His chest was a brewer's barrel,
His body massed muscle.

It was not sadness
I saw in his eye, nor madness,

But quiet resignation; he stood
Quite still, then ambled off. His food

Was almost due;
There was nothing for him to do

With his hard intricate feet,
With his head, that granite block,

But stand and wait.
It was a disgraceful waste

Of vitality and power.
'But if you'd not seen him there,'

My friend reminded me,
'Then you might never see

A prairie buffalo.'
This is perhaps true.

I might never see this creature
And that would be far better.

The Bear

Chained to his pole, the dancing bear
Waltzes across the village square.

His keeper skips along the middle
Scraping a tune on an old cracked fiddle.

With leather boots and scarlet shirt
He leads the creature through the dirt.

The great beast lumbers round and round
While coins are flung upon the ground.

Pity the clumsy dancing bear
Who used to breathe the forest air.

The White Mouse

my
  eye
is a wink!
  a whisk
  my
    frisk-
        y
        tail;
    my
        pink
feet
      spread
under
    my
few
  ounces
i
    sit
  upright
    and hold
my feed
      be
        tween
           my
        fingers.

my drink
   i nuzzle.
inqu-
     is-it(?)
         ive
i am
  and twitchy.
i sleep
      and wake
to my
    own
   small rhythms.
i stare
      blink
and am

     gone.

Twink!

Duffy

The white cat furies
In a squirm of purring.

He writhes in his delight,
Rolling his restless head
He tunnels my ready lap.

He loops his length
Hooping his lithe spine.

The white cat settles,
Licks at a stiffened leg,
Then sleeps — a lazy shape.

The white cat dreams of snow fields,
The small musical pipes of birds,
Licking his lips in sleep.

Grace Our Tabby-blonde

Grace, our tabby-blonde, whose plump 'murraoo!'
Conveyed such subtle shades of meaning,
    Has left us now.
Of late beside the fire she'd socialize,
Stretching her claws, or, indolently preening,
    Blink her slow eyes.

Time was, her style of manners was less nice,
When tribute from the garden she would fetch
    Of headless mice
Or ravaged finch. Agent she was for Death,
Who now, without remorse, ungrateful wretch,
    Has stopped her breath.

Scene

On the steaming dung
of horses and cows,
glittering like winged jewels,
the flies feast;

perfecting his web
beside the barn door
Sir Spider prepares to dine
on fed flies,

till Tib our quaint cat
smashes him with a blow,
who will later lie purring
on mother's lap.

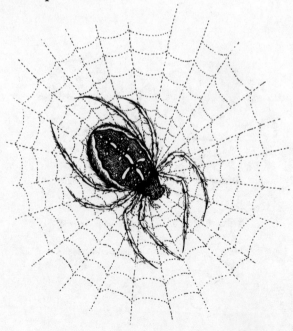

Araneus Diadematus

Agile I am, a high-wire walker.
A skilful ropemaker.
I can abseil downward
Or climb improbably through the air.

I am a patient waiter,
A swift runner, a heartless poisoner,
An architect of fantastic geometries,
A complicated dancer.

There are some who fear me
Among the fleshy bipeds,
My plump body scares them,
My eight angle-poised legs.

Or perhaps it is an idea
That fills them with terror —
That I may have a mind.
That I, too, have a maker.

Ant Number 1,049,652

Like a small yacht over a sea of grass
He tacks, carrying a green sail of leaf.

On the goad of his own acid he hastes
To receive or bestow a merciless death.

War machine directed by an unseen commander,
Minute mobile bottle of lethal chemical.

His mind lies outside his body. He is a fury
Of unbending purpose. The leaf will be delivered.

Wasp

A slim city slicker, sharp
In his black and yellow outfit,
He fines to a point of venom;
Winged singer, ruthless marauder
Whose soft head radiates fear.
God's pleasure in his workmanship
Is nowhere clearer to be seen
Than in this sleek visitor
To picnic and summer kitchen —
Perfect, beautiful and deadly.

Crawling on glass he is clumsy, a fumbler;
His mastery is shown in the air,
Riding without effort, landing on a jam pot.
He can patrol a straight line
Inches above the floor.

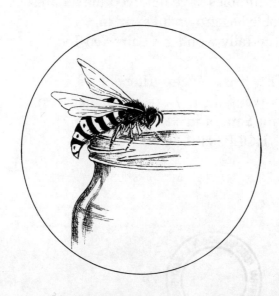

Hlep

Something has gone wrog in the garden.
There are doffadils blooming in the nose-beds,
And all over the griss dandeloons
Wave their ridigulous powdered wigs.

Under the wipping willop, in the pond
Where the whiter-lollies flute,
I see goldfinches swamming
And the toepaddles changing into fargs.

The griss itself is an unusual shade of groon
And the gote has come loose from its honges.
It's all extrepely worlying!
Helg me, some baddy! Heap me!

And it's not unly in the ganden.
These trumbles have fellowed me indares.
The toble has grown an extra log
And the Tally won't get Baby-See-Too.

Even my trusty Tygerwriter
Is producing the most peaqueueliar worms.
Helg me Sam Biddy. Kelp me!
Helg! HOLP! HELLO! !

Index of First Lines